THIS WALKER BOOK BELONGS TO:

_____

_____

_____

To Adam
S. MᶜB.

To Eden, with love
I. B.

First published 1998
by Walker Books Ltd
87 Vauxhall Walk
London SE11 5HJ

This edition published 2003

10 9 8 7 6 5 4 3

Text © 1998 Sam MᶜBratney
Illustrations © 1998 Ivan Bates

The right of Sam MᶜBratney and
Ivan Bates to be identified as author
and illustrator respectively of this
work has been asserted by them
in accordance with the Copyright,
Designs and Patents Act 1988

This book has been typeset
in Golden Type

Printed in China

British Library Cataloguing
in Publication Data:
a catalogue record for this book is
available from the British Library

ISBN 0-7445-9817-6

www.walkerbooks.co.uk

Sam McBratney

Just You and Me

Illustrated by Ivan Bates

WALKER BOOKS
AND SUBSIDIARIES
LONDON · BOSTON · SYDNEY · AUCKLAND

Once there was a little gosling goose and her name was **Little Goosey.**

One day **Little Goosey** and **Big Gander Goose,** who looked after her, set out to walk down to the river.

They hadn't gone far when the wind began to blow.
Gander **G**oose looked up at the dark clouds racing
across the sky and said, "A storm is coming.

We'd better find a place to hide."
"A nice warm place? Just for me
and you?" said **L**ittle **G**oosey.
"Just us," said **G**ander **G**oose.
"A place where we can rest
until the storm is over."
And they hurried into the
woods, looking for a place to hide.
"Will there be thunder when the
storm comes?"asked **L**ittle **G**oosey.
"Well, yes, there could be some thunder,"
said **G**ander **G**oose.

Soon they found a hole in a ditch, but there was
someone in there already – a small, grey-whiskered
mouse. She was hiding from the storm, too.
"You can stay in here with me if you like,"
said the mouse.

Little Goosey whispered
to Gander Goose:
"I don't want anybody else
when the thunder comes.

Just me and you."

Gander Goose thanked the small, grey-whiskered mouse. "It's a bit too damp in here for us," he said. "You're very kind, but I think we'll look for somewhere else. Goodbye."

When the other two had gone, the mouse saw some wet moss growing up the walls.
"It *is* a bit damp in here," she thought to herself. "I'll look for a better place, too."

Gander **G**oose and **L**ittle **G**oosey went further
into the woods, looking for a place to hide. They
found a hole among the roots of a tall tree,
but there was someone in there already –
a squirrel with a high, proud tail.
"Would you like to stay in here with me?"
said the squirrel.

Little Goosey whispered to
Gander Goose:
"But I don't want anybody else.

Just me and you."

Gander Goose thanked the squirrel with the high, proud tail. "I can see daylight above our heads," he said. "You're very kind, but I think we'll look for somewhere else. Goodbye."

When the other two had gone, the squirrel looked up and saw the sky through the trunk of the hollow tree. "The rain *could* easily run in through that hole," he thought to himself. "I'll try to find a better place, too."

Little **G**oosey and **G**ander **G**oose ventured
further into the woods. They found an interesting
cave among the rocks, but a rabbit with
furry ears had found it before them.
"We could all stay here together if you like,"
said the rabbit.

Little Goosey nestled into the
soft feathers of Gander Goose, and said quietly:
"I don't want there to be anybody else
when the thunder comes.

Just me and you."

Gander Goose thanked the rabbit with furry ears.
"There are too many stones in here for us," he said.
"You're very kind, but I think we'll look for
somewhere else. Goodbye."

When the other two had gone, the rabbit couldn't
find a space to lie down properly.
"It *is* too stony in here," she thought to herself.
"I'll look for a better place, too."

Little **G**oosey was beginning to feel tired after
all that searching for a place to hide, but then they
found a hole behind a bush at the bottom of a hill.
"This looks like a good place to be out of the storm,"
said **G**ander **G**oose. "And there's no one here."

"Just us," yawned **L**ittle **G**oosey.
She made a tunnel under some blown-in leaves,
so that she wouldn't hear the thunder if it came,
and lay down to sleep.

The storm arrived.
A great wind blew through the
trees and the rain came down.
In the fields and in the woods no one
could be seen, for they were all
hiding from the storm.

The dark clouds passed over. The wind died
down and soon the skies were clear again.
Little **G**oosey blinked in the ray of
sunlight shining into the hole.
Then she heard someone behind her.

"This was a good place to hide from the storm,"
said the small, grey-whiskered mouse.
"It was," agreed the squirrel with the high, proud tail.
"A very good place to hide from the storm,"
said the rabbit with furry ears.

The mouse, the squirrel and the rabbit waved
goodbye, and then ran off into the woods.
"This was a good place to hide from the storm,"
laughed **L**ittle **G**oosey. "For all of us!"

Gander **G**oose looked out at the trees, still
dripping after all the rain. "It was. And now
I think we'll walk down to the river," he said.

"Just us?"
asked **L**ittle **G**oosey.
Gander **G**oose
smiled and said:

"Just you and me."

WALKER BOOKS is the world's leading
independent publisher of children's books.
Working with the best authors and illustrators
we create books for all ages, from babies
to teenagers – books your child will
grow up with and always remember. So…

FOR THE BEST CHILDREN'S BOOKS,
LOOK FOR THE BEAR